**IMAGINE THAT™**

Licensed exclusively to Imagine That Publishing Ltd
Tide Mill Way, Woodbridge, Suffolk, IP12 1AP, UK
www.imaginethat.com
Copyright © 2019 Imagine That Group Ltd
All rights reserved
4 6 8 9 7 5
Manufactured in China

Written by Stephanie Dragone
Illustrated by Louise Ellis

ISBN 978-1-78700-913-4

A catalogue record for this book is available from the British Library

# I Love my Mummy

Written by Stephanie Dragone
Illustrated by Louise Ellis

I LOVE MY MUMMY BECAUSE … in the morning she wakes me with a kiss and says, 'Wakey, wakey, rise and shine, All the moonbeams are in the jar.'

I LOVE MY MUMMY BECAUSE ...
when I ask why I don't have a tail
like Bongo, she replies,

'Because our tails became stories, like fairy tales.'

I LOVE MY MUMMY BECAUSE ... when we see the school bus turn the corner, she winks at me and starts singing,

'The wheels on the bus
go round and round,
Round and round,
Round and round.'

I LOVE MY MUMMY
BECAUSE ... when she
pushes me on the swing
she pretends to catch
my toes and we sing,

'Swinging up and down in my great big swing,
Swinging up and down in my great big swing.'

And then she grabs me and sings loudly,

'Won't you be my darling?'

I LOVE MY MUMMY BECAUSE ... when I run onto the football pitch she shouts,

'Have fun, play hard, I love you.'
Later she asks …
'Did you have fun? I am so proud of you.'

I LOVE MY MUMMY BECAUSE ...
she puts notes in my lunch box
that make me laugh.

'You are the *apple* of my eye.
I'm going *bananas* over you.
I hope you have a really *grape* day.'

I LOVE MY MUMMY BECAUSE … she gives me dough to make pizza for dinner and we sing,

'Eating pizza - so much fun,
Eating pizza - yum, yum, yum.'

I LOVE MY MUMMY BECAUSE ... when I'm in the bath she covers her eye with my pirate patch and says in a deep voice,

'Lets search the waves
For silver stars,
To decorate
Our moonbeam jars.'

We both laugh because
she sounds so funny.

I LOVE MY MUMMY BECAUSE ...
when our neighbour tells her
that I have my boots on the
wrong feet she just says,

'I know!' and winks at me.

She's proud of me because I can dress myself.

I LOVE MY MUMMY BECAUSE … after my bedtime story she kisses me and then whispers in my ear,

'Good night, sleep tight, don't let the bedbugs bite.'

We both giggle and then we let the moonbeams out of the jar.

# I LOVE MY MUMMY BECAUSE ...

Mummy and me are
on the same page.

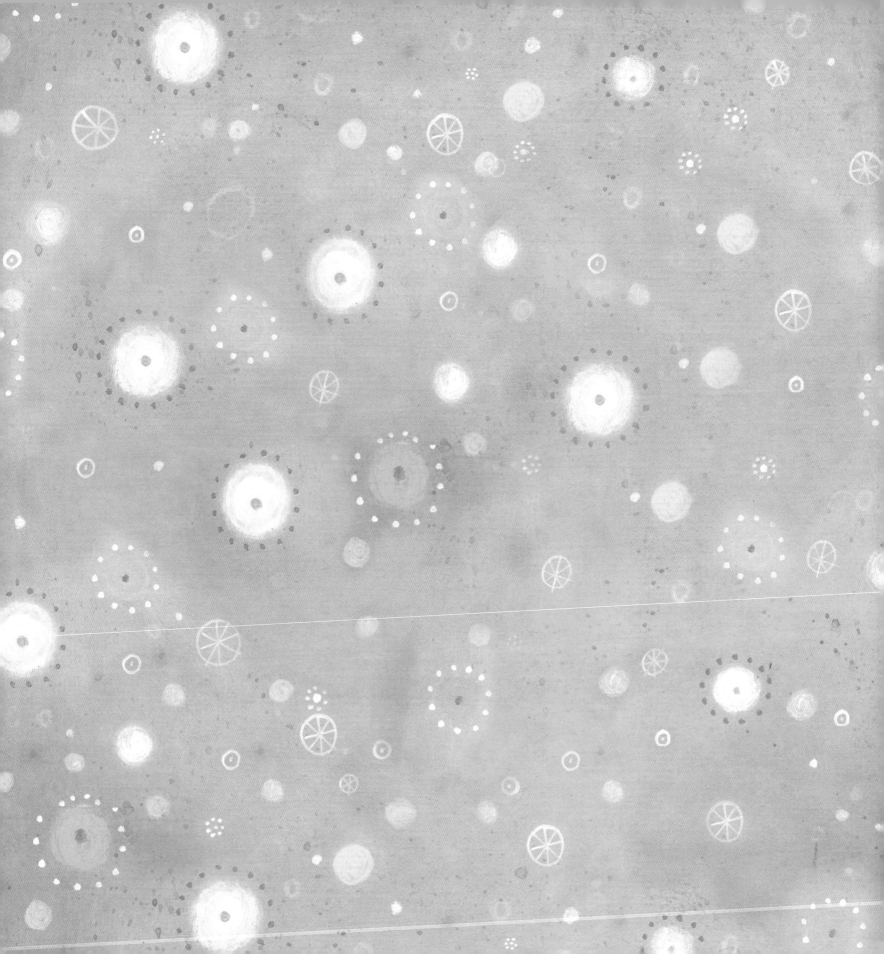

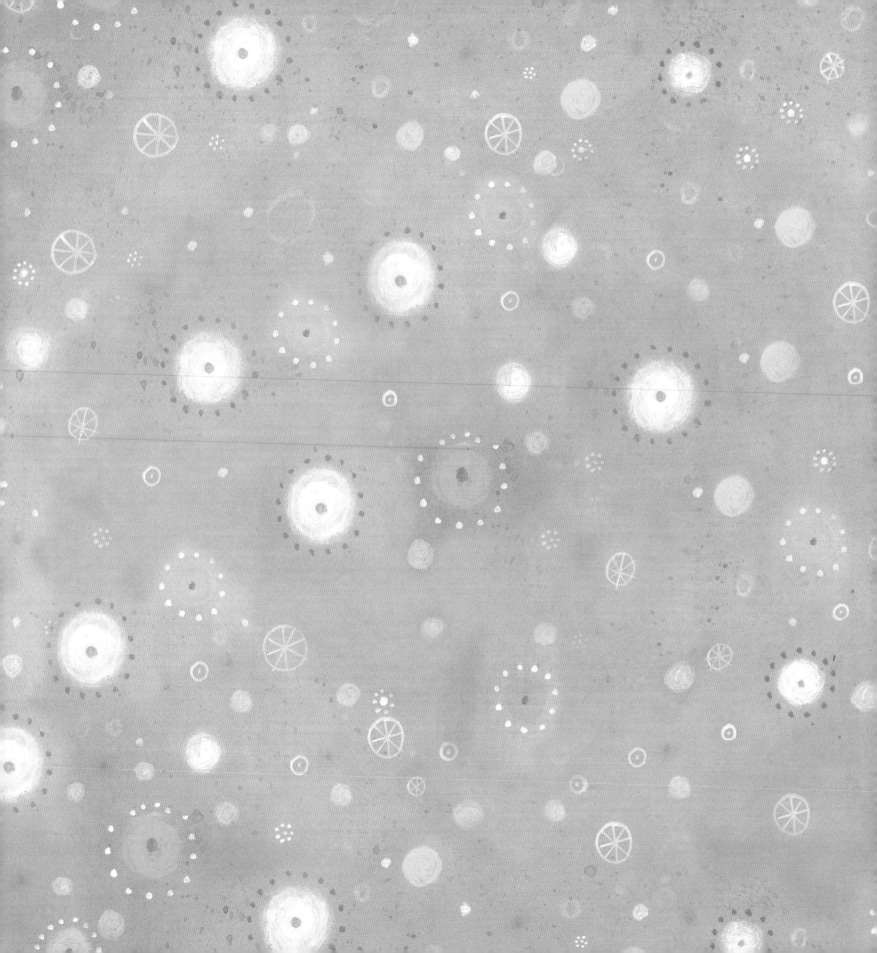